Contents

$\mathscr{L}$etter from the Editors

Welcome to the second edition of **Fearless Commerce**!

We are so grateful for all of the support received over the last year. The first edition was celebrated via numerous media outlets, in homes, schools, book clubs and the list goes on. This support has not only been for the book and the platform, but most importantly for the business owners. This is so amazing because above all else, this work was and continues to be about elevating Black women business owners. **Fearless Commerce** provides a beautiful space for them to be celebrated and for their story to be told.

Each of the Black women business owners were selected because they're bold and unafraid to push the limits in order to live life on their terms. They're working every day to transcend the social, cultural and economic barriers that may stand in their way. They've established businesses that are not only strengthening their families, they're also improving the overall quality of life in our communities.

Black women business owners are here and with investment, they will continue to have profound impact. As you flip through the pages, yes, you'll be met with nothing short of excellence, beauty and brilliance. We are blessed and honored to be stewards of this work through **Fearless Commerce**. We hope that you enjoy learning about the journeys of each of the women and of course, support their business!

Fearlessly,

Shawntera & Camille

Karen DeYoung

DeYoung Consulting Services
www.deyoungconsultingservices.com

Please describe your business: Our consultants are experts in helping get the job done more efficiently. We provide organizations with the insights they need to impact the systems, communities and environments in which they work. We provide organizational development, employee performance management, and evaluation services so organizations can more effectively achieve their mission. We have a niche of working with underrepresented communities. Additionally, we assess organizational challenges, acting as an outside facilitator who can look at the context from a knowledgeable, yet objective perspective. We'll serve as facilitator, organizer, and reporter to provide a clear, concise, and comprehensive final analysis, along with actionable recommendations.

What led your decision to start your business? I've been running my business for 20 years, though during the first 10 years I worked part time. I think I'm like a lot of entrepreneurs; I began this business because of the flexibility, being my own boss and being in charge of my own destiny. I did some consulting when I was in graduate school and took a fulltime job once I graduated. After being laid off, I realized I missed the flexibility and autonomy that I had with consulting. Over the years the firm has grown to include many team members with their own area of expertise.

What keeps you going? What drives you? I'm very fortunate to do work that is aligned with my passions. Collaboration with peers who share similar values with respect to integrity, an abundance mentality, high quality services, and a global perspective is what has kept me in the consulting business for so long. I love working with other people. While it's important to share values, creativity and innovation are borne by sharing diverse perspectives. I know that as human beings we hate change. I depend on outside perspectives to take me beyond "this is the way we've always done it."

How would you describe your brand? I've deliberately chosen to work with nonprofits and government agencies. I like the idea of doing high-quality, beyond expectations work for organizations that work to benefit communities in need.

What is your vision for your business? DeYoung Consulting Services to be known as a premier consulting firm specializing in organizational development and talent management. Though currently my clients are local, I would like our consulting services to be national, including work with the federal government.

What would you tell your younger self about entrepreneurship? Entrepreneurship is worthy of pursuing and will be seen as a badge of honor. Everyone is supposed to have at least a side hustle. Not so when I started. I didn't have role models for entrepreneurship in my family. My parents had "good gubment" jobs; and people often thought of consulting as something to pursue when you're between jobs. But I have a viable business that affords me a great salary while I do good work.

What would you say is your greatest professional accomplishment to date? May of 2011, the Midwest Minority Supplier Development Council (MMSDC) awarded DeYoung Consulting Services the Supplier of the Year Award for 2010, which is for businesses that consistently provide high quality products and contribute to the growth and development of society and their community. Most recently I was accepted into the competitive Small Business Administration's Emerging Leaders Initiative, which provides free entrepreneurship education and training for executives of small, poised-for-growth companies that are potential job creators. Admission required a certain amount of revenue. The program includes nearly 100 hours of classroom time and a chance to work with coaches and develop connections.

Eri O'Diah

Collective.ly Digital, LLC
www.collectivelydigital.com

Please describe your business: Collective.ly Digital is a new age digital marketing firm founded in 2013. Our unique partnership model allows us to deliver world-class digital marketing, print and technology solutions. Clients don't get a "one size fits all" solution from us. We offer tailored digital marketing, backed by solid data and research, that contributes directly to the clients' business growth.

What led your decision to start your business? The decision to start my own business was directly influenced by my need to take control over my professional trajectory and financial freedom. After years of being overlooked and undervalued in corporate America, I came to the realization that as a person of color, I may never attain the level of success I aspire to gain due to the deep systematic racism that prevailed across corporations in the United States.

What keeps you going? What drives you? I've been told by various people throughout my life that I was either not intelligent, not talented, not creative, ugly or simply not enough. What keeps me going and drives me is the fact that I'm defying all the adversities and have not succumbed to naysayers. I want to be a positive example to others who either suffer from low self-esteem, economically challenging backgrounds and/or depression.

How would you describe your brand? Collective.ly Digital is comprised of dreamers, travelers and seasoned professionals united by a passion for creating unforgettable digital experiences. We develop strategically aligned campaigns that move our clients' businesses towards a single goal. With partners from vastly diverse verticals, we're never short of new ideas, unique perspectives and creative angles for our clients.

What is your vision for your business? My vision for Collective.ly Digital is to be the preferred external marketing team for small, medium and large sized companies here in Minnesota and globally. I'd also like to position my brand as the destination for talented remote workers looking for opportunities to showcase their skills, collaborate with peers and produce award winning campaigns.

What would you tell your younger self about entrepreneurship? I would tell my younger self that entrepreneurship requires great sacrifices. You're working 24/7 and the term "my own boss" is a facade as you are an employee of your client. Without clients, you have no business. Invest early in business development skills and coaching in your entrepreneur journey.

What would you say is your greatest professional accomplishment to date? My greatest professional accomplishment to date is the successful launch of Collective.ly Digital. My brand is thriving due to solely word of mouth referrals. We've had the great fortune of providing services to the 2018 MN Super Bowl Host Committee, NFL Business Connect, and driving strategy at the Minnesota State Systems level.

"What keeps me going and drives me is the fact that I'm defying all the adversities and have not succumbed to naysayers."

Joi Thomas

Red Cricket Healing Center
www.redcricket.com

Please describe your business: Red Cricket Healing Center is a full-service health care clinic. The issues we most commonly treat are digestive disorders, women's health, dermatological disorders, and emotional challenges like anxiety and depression. Our approach stems from the belief that when people are confronted with illness it will show itself in all areas of their life – physical, emotional and spiritual. My patients' ability to thrive in this world is enhanced by a healthy body and mind, so that they can fully and without reservation bring their sacred light into this world and fulfill their sacred purpose.

What led your decision to start your business? I've always been drawn to be a healer since I was a little girl. But my deepest inspiration is true healing – health that transforms lives. When I graduated from my higher education program in Chinese Medicine, there was no structure for this kind of healing work in hospitals. So I had to hug myself really hard to strengthen my heart and start my own gig. It was my drive to transform lives and communities through health and healing that made me move through my fears and drive forward to set a good example for my children.

What keeps you going? What drives you? My parents raised my brothers and me to use our gifts to create a better world. I decided that the way I do that is by reuniting my patients with the power and beauty within them. If they feel empowered they will support peace and goodness in this beautiful world in their own special way. I see the good I do in my clinic blossoming like lovely flowers all over our community and our world.

How would you describe your brand? Love. Love is the true healer, and I try to align myself with the most powerful force available! Love makes me work harder and continue to educate myself. Love creates true healing, and I think people know that in their hearts. They know that they aren't a machine that needs to be fixed, but a sacred being created out of and fueled by love. There can be no true healing without love.

What is your vision for your business? This is a very exciting time for me personally. As I enter midlife and evaluate my future, I am moved to do the same with my business. I am beginning to reach full capacity, so I plan to move towards other modes of healing and teaching that will reach more people more efficiently, like working with groups in workshop settings and through writing. But I will always hold my patient work close to my heart, so that will always be a part of my work life.

What would you tell your younger self about entrepreneurship? I would tell her to buckle her seatbelt and be prepared to grow spiritually! No one ever told me how spiritual enriching owning a business could be. Being able to make a living by creating a business fueled by my joy is a very beautiful and wondrous thing.

What would you say is your greatest professional accomplishment to date? Every patient is my greatest accomplishment, because any bit of suffering I can take away from this planet is a miraculous thing. This means that my days are filled with miracles – and one miracle is never more or less important than another! My job is a deep and profound blessing!

Raeisha & Rosemary Williams

Heritage Tea House Boutique
www.facebook.com/TheHeritageTeaHouse

Please describe your business: **Raeisha**: Heritage Tea House is a restaurant, teahouse, and cabaret that honors and celebrates the History and Heritage of African Americans in Minnesota. We offer a full range of dining options (soul food, panini's, rice bowls), pastries, and beverages ranging from tea (over 20 flavors) coffee, fresh smoothies. We host weekly entertainment such as our: Speakeasy Open Mic; TGIF Happy Hour; Frogtown Comedy; Soul Saturday's featuring a live Band and Sunday Soul Brunch. **Rosemary**: The Tea House is a hisorical representation of the women in my family being in business in the Twin Cities. My mother had a cleaning service, and my grandmother was a seamstress.

What led your decision to start your business? **Raeisha**: I've always been a business woman. Prior to opening the Tea House, I owned other successful businesses; DF Media, a multi-service public relations/ marketing firm with a client roster that included Clear Way, Target, and super producer "Drumma Boy". Last year I opened a spa boutique called "The LashBar" which offered mink lash extensions and spa services. **Rosemary**: I wanted my children and grandchildren to have an inheritance. I believed that there was a community need to have more African American businesses, that would flourish and be supported by the black dollar.

What keeps you going? What drives you? **Raeisha**: The desire to have financial freedom, create job opportunities for African Americans, and create quality businesses that my community can value and appreciate. **Rosemary**: A desire to build a black economic platform for generations to come in the Twin Cities.

How would you describe your brand? **Raeisha**: Beverly Hills in the Hood. My business model is to create elegant spaces that offer high-quality service and products right in the heart of the African American community. **Rosemary**: A place to come to eat, drink, and buy African/African American culture gift items.

What is your vision for your business? **Raeisha**: To expand within the next year by opening a second location in the Twin Cities and in the future opening operations in other parts of the country. **Rosemary**: To expand the business and create another location in Minneapolis.

What would you tell your younger self about entrepreneurship? **Raeisha**: Be patient! Take time out for you! Love on yourself with self-care! **Rosemary**: Learn all you can about your business and be informed as much as possible about the business.

What would you say is your greatest professional accomplishment to date? **Raeisha**: I don't believe that I've reached this point in my life. I will breathe and say well done Raeisha when my family wants for nothing (monetarily) and we're able to begin our family foundation that will support in uplifting our community. **Rosemary**: The Tea House - Getting our prime location, the financing, and opening our doors.

Sarah Moe

Sleep Health Specialists
www.sleephs.com

Please describe your business: Sleep Health Specialists provides sleep health education to local businesses and corporations, creating healthier, happier, and more productive teams.

What led your decision to start your business? After 10 years in the field of Sleep Medicine working as a Board registered sleep technologist and Adjunct Professor in Polysomnography, I realized that I was continually having the same conversation with members of my community. Upon disclosing that I worked in "Sleep", complete strangers would begin a personal & intimate conversation with me in attempts to gain some knowledge into how to get a better night sleep.

So many of us are suffering from fatigue due to lack of sleep and sleep education. I realized it was time for me to do something about it. I decided to start a wellness company that connected what I loved and helping people, most importantly our workforce, feel better!

What keeps you going? What drives you? I am fueled by gratitude. Every class I teach is followed by countless emails saying, "Thank You." Thank you for coming to my office, thank you for teaching me about sleep disorders and thank you for helping save my spouses life. It's incredibly humbling and rewarding to be able to have a positive impact in a person's life in that way. It's hard to put into words the feeling that this feedback gives me. Knowing that I was able to help someone feel better leads to more joy in their lives and drives me.

How would you describe your brand? I hope that I and my company's brand mirror each other - caring, fun, compassionate, and most importantly, impactful. Sleep medicine can be serious- life threatening in fact- but it can also be revolutionary, which is fascinating and fun. Sleep Health Specialists stands for positive change, and we feel fortunate every day to be able to have that impact on our community.

What is your vision for your business? We hope to continue working with local corporations and businesses to get our community operating on full blast! Once Minnesota is sufficiently well rested, we will continue our work across the country.

What would you tell your younger self about entrepreneurship? I would tell myself that being an entrepreneur is hard on every level. The perseverance needed is almost unimaginable. You will have 20 fails for every win, experience guilt, remorse, doubt and despair at every turn, and constantly wonder if you've made a terrible mistake in believing in yourself. And then, after all the anguish, you will be amazed that what you do will pay off and success will come. It will be such a sweet, sweet sense of accomplishment that you'll forget all of the bad and wonder why you waited so long to start the journey.

What would you say is your greatest professional accomplishment to date? Being named one of the "Women Who Lead 2018" by the Minnesota Business Magazine was such an honor. The women accompanying me on that list are some of the most amazing ladies I've had the privilege of meeting!

"Once Minnesota is sufficiently well rested, we will continue our work across the country."

Jasmine McConnell

Butters By Jay
www.buttersbyjay.com

Please describe your business: Butters By Jay is a handmade natural bath and body personal care line with products formulated for multifunctional benefits. We create personal care products that that perform at least two functions such as intense penetrating moisture, cleansing, exfoliation and medicinal properties throughout all of our collections.

What led your decision to start your business? Butters By Jay stemmed from an eight year natural hair journey. After four years of purchasing products for my natural hair, I experienced that many of them were not meeting my need for a uniform style for my multi textured hair at a moderate price.

After 2 years of ongoing research on porosity of hair, soap making, and beneficial oils and ingredients for healthy skin and hair, I developed Butters By Jay in 2014. It was time to develop products for the public in a time where products were not readily available.

What keeps you going? What drives you? I truly believe in producing products "using natural ingredients to assist the body in a natural way"! Our skin is the largest organ that absorbs every day toxins. Bringing awareness and solutions to combat these issues is my servitude and contribution. There is a need for alternative natural moisturizers, soaps, scrubs, exfoliates and other personal care items and Butters By Jay is a line that is rooted in solutions. When I have customers sharing their testimonies of how a simple product of mine has changed their life in some way, I'm able to keep pushing pass hard decisions to keep formulating products as natural as possible.

How would you describe your brand? As consumers become increasingly interested in reading product labels, they're demanding products that offer something unique and truly beneficial, Butters By Jay is a perfect fit. The spotlight has been placed on what products do not contain rather than the exceptional ingredients they do contain. Butters By Jay connects customers with their needs and creates the simplest yet most effective products.

What is your vision for your business? Butters By Jay vision is to be the healthy alternative to traditional products by creating products with natural ingredients and medicinal properties and without high levels of lye, perfumes, dyes and fewer preservatives. The beauty industry has made great strides in natural products, but there's opportunities for innovation. The good news is that this consumer challenge is driving innovation and giving consumers more options than ever before.

What would you tell your younger self about entrepreneurship? Entrepreneurship is a commitment to being uncomfortable at attaining your servitude to the world. Your dream is never too big until it scares you. If you stay consistent and clear on your goals, mountains will move out your way.

What would you say is your greatest professional accomplishment to date? The greatest professional accomplishment to date with Butters By Jay is I took a chance and betted on myself. We're gaining momentum each day and can stand behind studies of real beneficial results from the daily use of Shea butter and other natural derivative base ingredients we formulate.

Khadija Ali

Global Language and Staffing Connections
www.globallanguageconnections.com

Please describe your business: Global Language and Staffing Connections is a language and staffing services company that works with for profit and nonprofit companies to facilitate opportunities and improve outcomes for the clients and customers they serve.

What led your decision to start your business? I have always wanted to operate a business since I was a young girl. My mom was an entrepreneur and I saw her lead her company. She worked hard to ensure its success.

I believe that profitable businesses can create greater wealth in families and in the community. From my experience, I know that this can be done and done effectively by creating connections and cultural agility between diverse communities. I also wanted to be an example and inspiration for young women of color.

What keeps you going? What drives you? I'm driven by the people and varies communities that we serve. Despite barriers, they continue to move forward. Most importantly, my two daughters keep me going in this work. I want to be a role model for them just as my mom was a role model for me.

How would you describe your brand? I would describe our brand as Global, Fresh, Authentic and Approachable.

What is your vision for your business? The vision for Global Language and Staffing Connections is to continue to cre-
ate connections for the greater good. If successful we will eliminate barriers and build connections between underrepresented immigrants and mainstream societies in order to build thriving communities. That's our vision and We believe that we can achieve it!

What would you tell your younger self about entrepreneurship? Trust yourself. Be patient. You can do it. Focus, Focus, and Focus some more.

What would you say is your greatest professional accomplishment to date? I would say that my greatest professional accomplishments include working with the 2018 Super Bowl 52 Host Committee. We were able to woark with them to bridge language issues. Overall, we've been able to prove our business model and over deliver to our clients and communities all while having a ton of fun.

"I believe that profitable businesses can create greater wealth in families and in the community. From my experience, I know that this can be done and done effectively by creating connections and cultural agility between diverse communities."

Rosemary Ugboajah

Neka Creative
www.nekacreative.com

Please describe your business: Neka Creative is a brand development firm, known for delivering smart solutions through our proprietary process of Inclusivity Marketing™. Inclusivity Marketing is the holistic approach of bringing different perspectives, histories, experiences, needs and motivations together in one cohesive brand development effort.

We bring this passionate commitment to every client and every single thing we do. As a result, our measure of success goes well beyond mere tactical resolution. We become an integral part of our clients' businesses, providing services that are as in-depth as they are inclusive, including: qualitative/quantitative research, strategic directions, identity development, brand campaigns, culture building and experiential engagement.

What led your decision to start your business? A strong desire to operate at my fullest potential in an environment that celebrates success while respecting individuals and valuing the wealth of our uniqueness. Before Neka Creative, I worked in a number of creative agencies and a large corporation. I learned a lot and gained a great deal of experience at each of these companies, but I found that many of them fell short of satisfying my personal and professional desire for that special place for people to shine. It became evident that if I wanted it, I had to build it.

What keeps you going? What drives you? I am driven by our mission to lead the industry through example, advancement and acknowledgement of an inclusive brand movement. I envision a time when the majority of organizations will be inclusive. Places where people of all backgrounds, abilities, orientations, ages and creeds will be able to thrive; not by conforming to the status quo but by being lifted up and valued for the unique contribution they make.

How would you describe your brand? Simply put, we are wild about building inclusive brands.

What is your vision for your business? We built our firm on the vision to "be the role model for inclusivity." That translates to aligning brands with powerful inclusive strategic directions. And above all, it's about understanding the need for all voices, cultures and people to be taken into deep consideration.

What would you tell your younger self about entrepreneurship? I would tell my younger self to overcome fear by doing. That owning a business will build your character and stretch your abilities in ways you could never imagine. That entrepreneurship will give you the freedom to make a true difference in the world. It will be liberating and exciting.

What would you say is your greatest professional accomplishment to date? Building an inclusive brand development firm is one of my greatest accomplishments, but I have to share that accomplishment with my team. They embody what it means to be inclusive. They respect and value each other. They genuinely care about seeing us, and our clients, succeed. This attitude and commitment consistently extends to the work we produce every single day.

Natalia Hals

A Woman's Design
www.awomansdesign.com

Please describe your business: A Woman's Design is the first full-service agency specializing in doula, childbirth, and family education services in Minneapolis and St. Paul. We provide comprehensive services in a caring, compassionate, knowledgeable, and professional manner.

What led your decision to start your business? I've always had the mindset of an entrepreneur, and I've never been content with a regular 9-5 job. I'm passionate about women's rights, wellness, and empowerment, and A Woman's Design is the result of this.

What keeps you going? What drives you? Running my own business has shown my three children what is possible in the world.

A Woman's Design allows me to create a space where all women can find their own greatness. I'm also a dreamer. Every morning I wake up with a fire in my belly to bring into being what I want to manifest in the world.

How would you describe your brand? A Woman's Design provides unparalleled education and support to mothers, their families and friends so that they are healthy, happy, and empowered during pregnancy, birth, and motherhood.

What is your vision for your business? Our vision is the Nesting Place, the next growth phase of A Woman's Design. It will be an office building in Roseville, Minnesota, that leases office space to service providers that support women during early conception, pregnancy and postpartum. We aim to reach this goal by creating a collaborative community with local caregivers, specialists, and support groups.

What would you tell your younger self about entrepreneurship? I would tell my younger self to not worry so much about failures. They do not have to define or destroy you. We can all learn and build off of our mistakes.

What would you say is your greatest professional accomplishment to date? My greatest professional accomplishment to date has been bringing my oldest daughter with me during events at which I've been recognized so she could see in person how with focus and determination, a young woman cut a path to success.

"I'm also a dreamer. Every morning I wake up with a fire in my belly to bring into being what I want to manifest in the world."

De'Vonna Pittman

Natures Syrup
www.naturesyrup.com

Please describe your business: Nature's Syrup specializes in creating products free of junk and chemicals. We focus on providing healthy skin and hair care solutions.

What led your decision to start your business? While seeking an alternative hair care product for my natural hair, I created a formula that not only worked miracles on my thick, coarse hair, but one that had amazing results on my skin. After countless hours of mixing shea butter and various oils, it was evident that the product left my skin silky smooth. Body Butter is our staple product, but we've mastered other heavenly concoctions that are also top sellers! I tested the market by offering products free to people in my circle and at my church and realized others wanted great products as well.

What keeps you going? What drives you? I challenge myself to do things I'm afraid of doing. I can live with someone saying no, I can't live with not doing. I'm driven by the sheer desire to prove to myself that I can do anything I put my mind to. This can be a challenge, especially when things don't always work out as expected. My family loves and believes in me, and they see me in ways no one does. I'm driven by their unfailing love. I pray the work I do to enhance lives resonates long after my work here is done. Ever day is a gift, and if I'm not creating, managing projects, or writing, I'm not in a good place. The mere thought of not having enough time to do all the things I aspire is daunting. So I live each day as if it were my last and make every second count.

How would you describe your brand? It's humbling to have people rave about my products. Many have no idea the time and commitment it takes to formulate, blend, and package quality products through trial and error. By the time my product reaches the customer's hand, it has touched mine at least 50 times. Nature's Syrup was derived from a passion to create products with quality ingredients that work on all hair and skin types. People feel my heart and soul when they use Nature's Syrup.

What is your vision for your business? Our name definitely describes the vision and the accountability needed to stay true to its evolution. One of my customers perfectly penned our marketing phrase: "Nature's Syrup is the raw essence of nature unbridled." I was born and raised in poverty in the poorest suburb in America and was destined to be a statistic. I dropped out of high school and was a single parent by the time I was twenty. The odds were against me, but I overcame. As an author and public speaker my greatest desire is to speak to the masses about the tragedies and my journey to become an entrepreneur! Nature's Syrup will empower those around the country who don't believe in themselves or those who think their past has affected their future.

What would you tell your younger self about entrepreneurship? Work hard young and finish strong. Find a hobby, a hustle, do what you love to create several streams of income. Never give up, because usually when you get tired, you are really close to scaling up! Don't get entangled with the no, because the yes will prevail in due time. You will never be too old to start a business, and you will never not be smart enough. You have everything it takes to achieve your goals. Keep working to perfect what you start until you're at peace.

What would you say is your greatest professional accomplishment to date? Last year, I co-hosted the Minnesota Black Author's Expo where we created a sacred space for authors to showcase their work. It was a huge success! I've had the honor of hosting several fulfilling women empowerment events across the country. But I receive more when I can speak life into youth. These are the moments in which my professional and personal experiences collide. A few months ago, I facilitated a discussion with girls from the elementary school in my home town. I felt the weight of responsibility leading up to the event and the need to be transparent and effective. The girls were completely engaged the entire time, and when they made me promise to come back, I knew I had done what I was called to do!

Lisa Tabor

CultureBrokers® LLC
www.culturebrokers.com

Please describe your business: CultureBrokers helps organizations get immediate, measurable, and valuable results from their diversity, inclusion and equity efforts.

What led your decision to start your business? I held management positions in the for-profit and nonprofit sectors for much of my life. I experienced how all types of organizations said that they embraced diversity but ultimately failed to translate that value into results for their stakeholders. During my last two jobs, I had excellent opportunities to strengthen my ability to translate vision into action then into results. Those experiences gave me both the idea and the confidence to create my business.

What keeps you going? What drives you? Results – and the clients who demonstrate a commitment to getting them – keep me passionate about my business. Diversity, inclusion and equity work is hard. Finding creative ways to change the individual and organizational behaviors that drive entrenched disparities is mentally and emotionally challenging. But, it is impossible to stop trying once you see significant, sustained improvements in outcomes for marginalized groups of people.

Happily, more of the organizations reaching out to me are willing to make necessary changes so they can drive those improvements now versus in five or ten years.

How would you describe your brand? Bold, pioneering and results-oriented.

What is your vision for your business? I'd like my business to be the go-to company for diversity, inclusion and equity results at a national or even global level. The Diamond Inclusiveness System I have been developing over the last twelve years with the help of clients, colleagues and advisors, has the potential to transform the field. As far as I can tell, it's the only comprehensive, systematic, and holistic approach to eliminating disparities that exists today. To get to that goal, I have launched the system as a set of public programming and I am working with a writer on a book.

What would you tell your younger self about entrepreneurship? Honestly, nothing. I've always had an entrepreneurial mindset, even if I was not interested in having my own business. Everything has happened the way it should have/could have happened.

What would you say is your greatest professional accomplishment to date? My accomplishments are directly linked to those of my clients. The results that still reign supreme in my career so far are those we continue to get from the Ramsey County Juvenile Detention Alternatives Initiative (JDAI). After being faced with increasing over-population of youth in its detention center, and mounting pressure from communities of color to reassess a system that disproportionately detained youth of color, Ramsey County launched an effort to change juvenile justice policies, processes, and situations in 2006.

Using the Diamond Inclusiveness System, I got to work with them to set up JDAI's organization and operational principles, systems and tools. Within the first year of implementation, Ramsey County reduced the inappropriate detention of youth (primarily children of color) by 10%. Seven years later, they maintain a daily population 70% lower than when they started. And, the rate of serious crimes has gone down by 27%.

It is gratifying to know that my work continues to help the county change outcomes for thousands of young people, mostly kids of color.

Anna Ouattara

Knowlogistics Consulting LLC
www.knowlogisticsedu.com

Please describe your business: Knowlogistics Consulting, L.L.C. is an advisory and training organization that specializes in Domestic/Global Transportation and Trade Compliance. We help businesses minimize their supply chain risks by assessing their current processes and providing better practices.

What led your decision to start your business? I decided to start Knowlogistics Consulting, L.L.C for a couple of reasons. The first reason was that I wanted my freedom to spend more time with my family at home. The second reason was I wanted to empower business owners and companies with the dos and don'ts of doing international business so that they can make better decisions and be successful. I wanted to be a solution to their need. The third reason was that no person of color, that I am aware of, does global logistics and trade compliance and there is a strong need for representation in the field.

What keeps you going? What drives you? My family keeps me going. I want them to be proud and also remind them to always strive for greatness. I want to challenge myself and believe that anything is possible. I also believe that we all have a purpose in life, and mine is to help others by using my skills. My drive is that time is more valuable than money, so I must make it count as tomorrow is not promised.

How would you describe your brand? This is a great question. I would say my brand is bold. I am not afraid to take risk and stay true to myself.

What is your vision for your business? My vision for my business is to be the vessel of trade solutions for clients globally.

What would you tell your younger self about entrepreneurship? I would tell my younger self to have faith, confidence and not allow fear to hinder you from your passion. I would tell my younger self to stay disciplined, be patient, and take the time to enjoy the journey. I would tell my younger self that you define your success.

What would you say is your greatest professional accomplishment to date? This is a really hard question. I would say starting my own business, teaching and starting my doctoral journey. I took the risk to follow my passion, empower others journey as we exchange knowledge in the classroom. I am excited, and I am grateful for my blessings.

"My drive is that time is more valuable than money, so I must make it count as tomorrow is not promised."

Dr. Sheila Sweeney

Peaces 'n PuzSouls
www.peacesnpuzsouls.org

Please describe your business: The mission of Peaces 'n Puz-Souls is to provide individualized and quality psychotherapy to individuals, families, and communities with diverse challenges. Our services include: Individual, Family, and Group Psychotherapy; Mental Health Assessments; PsychoEducation; Consulting and Reflection. Peaces 'n PuzSouls uses a variety of models including Biopsychosocial, Psychodynamic, and Strengths Perspective with a goal of empowerment, to assist individuals and communities to achieve the highest quality of life. Cultural practices and spiritual beliefs are welcome to holistically examine the background of each individual.

What led your decision to start your business? I've always had a desire start a business, but job security was difficult to let go. I was not truly satisfied with my current situation and it was better to take a financial risk than to stay where I did not feel 100% complete. Knowing my practice would one day become a reality; I paid attention to every detail in every job held. I took pride in my entry level positions, walking away with an understanding of good customer service and the ability to work with various families/cultures; and in my most senior positions, I left knowing that I mastered my craft.

These positions have led me to where I am today, I love the ability to create my own schedule and the freedom that goes along with it. This freedom feeds my passion and I'm able to share my knowledge with clients, students, agencies, colleagues and community. In owning my own business, I create my own destiny and take on responsibilities that speak to my heart. Entrepreneurship is in the DNA from both sides of my family and I am so proud to carry on this legacy.

What keeps you going? What drives you? I love what I do period! (she smiles)

How would you describe your brand? Integration, Relation and Interpretation. In my work, my brand cannot be separated from myself. Therefore, my brand is relational, caring, empathic, and authentic. I meet people where they are with a mutual baseline of respect, honesty, and professionalism.

What is your vision for your business? I want a holistic wellness, healing, intergenerational space. I need my practice and contribution to act as a container for healing. This will give people back the missing pieces to their puzzle, which is where my business name is birthed. It is my hope that everyone who comes for healing, leaves with peace. This is the triadic work between the therapist, the client, and the space that holds the energy/data that takes place in the room. Ultimately, I envision a consortium of clinicians working under one roof bringing interdisciplinary practices with rich skills and knowledge.

What would you tell your younger self about entrepreneurship? Don't be afraid. Start sooner. Believe in self. Find passion. Don't let anyone dim your light. Don't shrink. Delegate. Focus. Thrive in your life's work. My dad always told me "when you find a job you love, you will never work another day in your life." I live that.

What would you say is your greatest professional accomplishment to date? ME. Not shrinking. Becoming Dr. Sheila Roby Sweeney. I am comfortable in owning who I am today. I earned it, I feel it, I respect it, I am it! The TIME is right now and I am ready like never before. What God has for me is for me!

Nicole Jennings

Queen Anna House of Fashion
www.queenanna.co

Please describe your business: Queen Anna is a women's high end, contemporary fashion house that caters to independent designers. We partner with elite luxury lifestyle brands for women of all shapes and sizes.

What led your decision to start your business? The journey to Queen Anna began because of the loss of my great grandmothers. It was an outlet for me during my grieving process. The space is a continuation of a legacy left by them and an opportunity for me to do the same for my children. Additionally, it aligns with my personal love for fashion!

What keeps you going? What drives you? The thing that keeps me going as a business owner is the legacy that was created by my great grandmother which is continuing on through my work at Queen Anna.

I'm driven by the fact I was able to bring this new idea to reality. The words you can't or you won't push me to defy the odds. Lastly, I've seek to a role model for my family. My children are able to see first-hand and know that mommy did it and they can do it too.

How would you describe your brand? Queen Anna has an elevated perception of beauty, fashion, and philanthropy. We curate a contemporary NYC SoHo feel from our contemporary aesthetic and independent designers. The leading luxury lifestyle brand that is experienced based.

What is your vision for your business? The vision for Queen Anna is to create solid roots here in Minneapolis, and then venture out into other states and create roots there as well.

What would you tell your younger self about entrepreneurship? If I could tell my younger self anything as an entrepreneur, it would be to build a supporting cast that is in alignment with YOUR vision. Never rush and never settle.

What would you say is your greatest professional accomplishment to date? My greatest professional accomplishment to this date would be taking a blank lifeless building and creating a magnificent masterpiece called Queen Anna.

"I do what I do, not because I can, but because it's my calling. I have been granted the precious gift of life because I am supposed to impact the lives of others, so they can boldly and courageously walk into their life calling regardless of what the world around them may say. I believe I am a small part of God's greater plan for humanity and I refuse to let anyone stop me from doing my part.

I never do anything mediocre because I believe if you're going to do something you do it to the best of your ability. It's easy to be basic, you have to be dedicated and consistent to be great. Hard work beats talent, when talent doesn't work hard."

Nicole Pacini

Minneapolis Entréepreneur
nicolepacini.com

Please describe your business: Minneapolis Entréepreneur is a blog designed to showcase the culinary life in the Twin Cities as well as assist small businesses, culinarians, and non-profit organizations to increase their brand awareness and social media impact.

What led your decision to start your business? In 2012, I created a food blog titled The Entréepreneur to host the hundreds of photographs that I had collected of food over years of traveling and dining out. The following year I joined a health and wellness network marketing company after being unemployed for over a year.

Being able to work a home-based business allowed me to explore entrepreneurship and the benefits of earning income in a nontraditional manner. There was a huge sense of accomplishment and freedom when I made the decision to take control of what I wanted and what I needed in order to achieve my personal definition of success. Minneapolis Entréepreneur was formed in 2017 - combining my entrepreneurial spirit, infatuation with food and love of photography.

What keeps you going? What drives you? I am driven by the idea that my work is never complete. I have stories to share, people to inspire and children to leave a legacy.

How would you describe your brand? Nicole Pacini is the real brand. Nicole Pacini is bold, creative, outgoing, forward thinking and passionate about life.

Most people identify me as the social media fanatic who loves food and knows how to spark interesting dialogue. The Minneapolis Entréepreneur is the evolving brand of Nicole Pacini.

What is your vision for your business? My vision for Minneapolis Entréepreneur is to travel the world and work with culinarians of all classifications to help them build their brand and social media impact.

What would you tell your younger self about entrepreneurship? I am an Aries and have always been attracted to how we are defined. We are Enterprising, Spontaneous, Daring, Courageous, Adventurous, Pioneering and Confident. The perfect Entrepreneur!

What would you say is your greatest professional accomplishment to date? Taking action, believing that each failure and struggle that I have faced has been a stepping stone to my accomplishments and allowing myself to do things afraid. I published my first 30-day self-discovery journal in 2017, Not a Cloud in the Sky. It's full of intentional, daily assignments designed to impact how you view yourself, the world and the people around you.

"There was a huge sense of accomplishment and freedom when I made the decision to take control of what I wanted and what I needed in order to achieve my personal definition of success."

Melanie C. Lewis

The Perfect Piece Sweets Co.
perfectpiecesweets.com

Please describe your business: The Perfect Piece Sweets Co. is a premier dessert catering company specializing in mini desserts and custom cakes. All pieces are custom made using the highest quality ingredients and local suppliers to ensure that every piece is fresh and perfect. We are committed to creating beautiful desserts with exceptional, balanced flavors while delivering top-notch customer service.

What led your decision to start your business? I was tired of being comfortable. I knew there was more written to my life story than what I was living. Having a gift means nothing if there is no direction or purpose behind it. On December 30, 2015 I left my job in pursuit of my purpose.

What keeps you going? What drives you? When you have been given a purpose and vision you can't be stopped. I have a destination now, so no matter the rejections, I still know what I am supposed to be doing and I am convinced that it will work out for my good.

How would you describe your brand? I use my food as a tool to create experiences and memories. I like being able to get to know my clients in order to add those personal touches to their cake or dessert.

What is your vision for your business? Opening a pastry shop on the northside of Minneapolis is definitely on my radar. Having a space that people can come in and get a great cup of coffee, a pastry and read the morning paper without having to leave their neighborhood is what I look forward to. I also plan to use my business to create opportunities for other young brown culinarians to showcase their talents.

What would you tell your younger self about entrepreneurship? I would tell my younger self to stride and not strive. A person striving is reaching for something they don't have or expending great effort, almost to the point of exhaustion. They focus so much of their energy on the future until they don't take time to truly live in the present.

However, a person who strides walks with long, decisive steps in a specified direction. That means they walk with intention and purpose. They may not reach their goals as quickly as their counterparts, but they have learned to pace themselves, direct their energy efficiently and appreciate the process.

What would you say is your greatest professional accomplishment to date? Over my 10 + year career in the culinary industry, I've been blessed to have a career working and learning from some of the top chefs in the Twin Cities, and meeting culinary legends such as Thomas Keller, Daniel Boulud, and Jose' Andres. These chefs are widely renowned who collectively own multiple restaurants, have written several books and have earned an array of awards. Their many accomplishments have greatly impacted my life and career.

However, my greatest accomplishment to date has been the decision to step out of my comfort zone and take all that I have learned to create a name and legacy of my own.

Natalie Johnson-Lee

Sisters in Power 365, LLC
www.sistersinpower365.com

Please describe your business: Sisters In Power 365, LLC leads with purpose and passion to provide quantifiable cost saving solutions to organizations. Additionally, we partner with various communities to develop and execute policies that improve the social and structural determinants of health.

Our priority areas are: Workforce & Economic Development, Social Justice, Advocacy & Public Policy and Personal Branding. This is achieved through coaching, customized training, group facilitation and strategic planning. We help people be successful where the work, play, pray and stay.

What led your decision to start your business? My passion has always been to help people live powerful lives through self-awareness. So, it was quite natural for me to help friends, family members, and associates to develop plans, create strategies, and solve a variety of problems to enhance their future. One day someone asked, "What's your fee?"and then I quickly realized I could get paid for what I was doing for free. A business was born.

What keeps you going? What drives you? My desire to leave a legacy for my children, grandchildren and future generations and the freedom to create a lifestyle of my choice.

How would you describe your brand? Leadership, Compassion and Integrity

What is your vision for your business? Increased focus on helping women to become politically astute and financially savvy. The goal is for them to reshape the economics and political landscape of their communities through business and social entrepreneurship.

What would you tell your younger self about entrepreneurship? Trust your gut and seek mentors who know how to recognize vision and believe in you. Remember failure is a rest stop and not your final destination. Find one person who thinks you are amazing and that just might be you. Believe and encourage yourself. Help others.

What would you say is your greatest professional accomplishment to date? Trusting and believing in myself and my abilities. With that, I've pioneered multiple businesses and community initiatives that continue to strive today.

"Remember failure is a rest stop and not your final destination."

Melissa Levingston

Major Body Fitness
www.majorbodyfitness.com

Please describe your business: Major Body Fitness is a boutique fitness studio located in St. Paul, Mn. The Studio is owned and operated by myself and I have three fitness instructors that assist with teaching. We offer a variety of class formats including indoor cycling, strength training, cardio dance classes, kickboxing and yoga. To compliment the fitness classes there's a variety of Life Style programs that are offered such as Boot Camp and The 30 Day Clean Eating Challenge. Although group exercise is what I offer primarily, I also offer personal training. And for those that are not able to physically make it to the studio for a class, I also offer online training through a station on my website where you can subscribe.

What led your decision to start your business? I decided to start my own business and open my own fitness studio after years of working at other gyms and fitness studios. Although, my classes were the most popular classes at most of these facilities I was often told by the manager that I needed to play less hip hop and rap music and that I couldn't be so creative with my exercise routines. I'm an artist that LOVES to create not to mention I LOVE hip hop, so I had to leave and create my own space.

What keeps you going? What drives you? I've been very fortunate to have developed an extremely beautiful community of women that are not only my members but are my friends. Many of them express to me on a daily basis how grateful they are to have me and my business in their lives. That's what keeps me going!

!How would you describe your brand? Major Body Fitness is a brand of fitness that is extraordinary. My brand caters to all fitness levels. My brand caters to mostly women and these women come from a large variety of fitness and cultural backgrounds. My members experience priceless memories in class while getting amazing results that change their lives. My brand teaches women to love their Mind, Body & Soul.

What is your vision for your business? Major Body Fitness will inspire people to live a fit and healthy lifestyle while making living a fit and healthy lifestyle a simple and enjoyable way of life.

What would you tell your younger self about entrepreneurship? Don't be scared, just go for it!! You can do it because you already have all the tools that you need to succeed within you!!

What would you say is your greatest professional accomplishment to date? Running a successful business for 4 years now while helping a lot of women to reach their health and fitness goals.

"I'm an artist that LOVES to create not to mention I LOVE hip hop, so I had to leave and create my own space."

Y. Elaine Rasmussen

Social Impact Strategies Group/ConnectUP! MN
www.socialimpactnow.com and www.connectupmn.com

Please describe your business: Founded in 2016, Social Impact Strategies Group, LLC (SISG) is a Black/Native, woman-owned, B-corp certified company driven by the mission of democratizing access to capital by/for people of color. To achieve its mission, SISG offers three services: 1) strategy development, measurement & analysis, 2) human-centered business development for entrepreneurs and 3) convenings and education workshops for investors and entrepreneurs.

SISG produces an annual entrepreneur ecosystem event called ConnectUP! MN Summit which bridges the 180 degrees of separation between local investors and entrepreneurs from overlooked and under-resourced communities. Additionally, SISG hosts a monthly podcast called Social Impact Now!

What led your decision to start your business? I noticed 3 glaring things 1) a disconnect in quality resources to meet the needs of entrepreneur of color 2) limited efforts to connect investors to entrepreneurs of color and 3) a siloed entrepreneur ecosystem. To use a baseball analogy, Minnesota has a LOT of great resources when you're on home base and want to get to 1st base. Also, there are great resources if you're on 3rd base and you want to round home plate. What our entrepreneur ecosystem is missing is resources and capital for entrepreneurs of color who want to get to grow their business and get from 1st to 2nd, and 2nd to 3rd base. I saw I had a network and experience to serve those gaps.

What keeps you going? What drives you? I'm inspired by the resilience of entrepreneurs of color. One Black-woman owned business recently told me she was considering closing her business and after talking with us and attending ConnectUP! MN, she got the courage and inspiration to keep going. When I hear an investor is now dedicating a portion of their portfolio to investing in entrepreneurs of color it reminds me why I do what I do. Finally, the love and passion of my staff and family keeps me going.

How would you describe your brand? The key elements that power our delivery of quality programs and services are: Motivating (We want you to achieve amazing goals by getting (and keeping) you excited and forward-moving); Connecting (Making things happen by knowing the right people & resources at the right time); and Human-centered (Keeping the whole YOU in every aspect of what we do. We offer our programs and services at nights/weekends, we provide childcare and meals).

What is your vision for your business? Grow SISG staff and our footprint through satellite offices across the state so we can be locally connected to entrepreneurs of color throughout Minnesota. We also want to replicate ConnectUP! in other cities. Finally, we want to create the ConnectUP! Integrated Capital Fund, that targets blended capital options for entrepreneurs of color--built on a cooperative model that includes opportunities for equity ownership in the portfolio of companies in the fund. We're currently fundraising to pilot the Fund.

What would you tell your younger self about entrepreneurship? You are smarter and stronger than you think you are! You can do this!

What would you say is your greatest professional accomplishment to date? I don't think my greatest professional accomplishment has happened yet. Everything builds on the foundation of what's come before and all the great work across the ecosystem. But if pressed, I would have to say producing the first ConnectUP! MN Summit in March 2018. It went from idea to reality in less than 9 months!

Dara Beevas

Wise Ink
www.wiseinkpub.com

Please describe your business: Wise Ink Creative Publishing is a boutique indie publishing agency partnering with authors to publish with quality, impact, and most of all, strategy. With backgrounds in both traditional and indie publishing, we see the values in both avenues and we bring our authors the best of both worlds.

Our process is 100% custom—no templates or packages for the authors we work with, because no book fits perfectly in a one-size-fits-all publishing and marketing plan. We also bring editors and designers from the traditional publishing world and traditional distribution partners to give our authors the competitive edge they need to compete. Plus, our authors get to join our supportive author community—a network of like-minded authors who also believe that indie publishing doesn't mean cutting corners.

What led your decision to start your business? I started Wise Ink because I believe that books can save lives, open doors and build bridges, especially in communities of color. As co-CEO of Wise Ink, I encourage authors to share powerful stories that ignite change, tolerance, and growth. I'm living my dream.

What keeps you going? What drives you? Ideas are meant to breathe beyond its creator, and I pride myself on working with some of the most creative minds in the world, guiding their ideas to real impact. This is why I wake up every morning.

How would you describe your brand? The Wise Ink brand is about community, purpose, and creating books with soul. I hope that when people say the words Wise Ink, or meet one of our authors, or read one of our books, they get a sense for our passion and commitment to the written word.

What is your vision for your business? I want Wise Ink to become one of the most successful media corporations known for helping people who want to change the world, transform minds, and bring more joy to the masses.

What would you tell your younger self about entrepreneurship? Jump first. Think about the consequences and risks later. You are worthy.

What would you say is your greatest professional accomplishment to date? Becoming a Bush Fellow was pretty cool. But publishing my first book was amazing! I got to experience the joy of becoming an author and it helped make me a more intuitive publisher.

"Ideas are meant to breathe beyond its creator, and I pride myself on working with some of the most creative minds in the world, guiding their ideas to real impact."

Roxane Battle

Roxane Battle, M.A., LLC
www.roxanebattle.com

Please describe your business: As a solo entrepreneur my business is all about spreading joy across multiple platforms. I launched this entrepreneurial journey 2017, after the national release of my memoir Pockets of Joy: Deciding to Be Happy, Choosing to Be Free which won several literary awards and became a best-seller on Amazon in multiple categories.

What led your decision to start your business? With the success of my book, I knew I had to do more. After decades of working around the country for major media corporations as a television news reporter and anchor, it was as if God had given me a new platform and calling - simply to help people find happiness, especially women struggling to meet the demands of work and family while carving out time for themselves.

Helping to ease the emotional suffering of others by providing them tools to find joy in life has become a passion of mine. Through speaking, book publishing, blogging, video projects and one-on-one mentoring sessions, I'm able to combine my life experiences as a professional journalist, with research on the science of happiness and provide candid insight on what it takes to be happy in life.

What keeps you going? What drives you? After decades of reporting on other people's stories, I am finally telling my story and to see the impact that true candor and authentic storytelling has on people is a huge motivator for me. Letting people know that you share their same experiences, understand their pain and that they're not alone in their struggles is very powerful.

Transparent storytelling has a way of breaking a person's isolation and setting them free on a path towards joy. I see this all the time when people come up to me after a presentation or during a book signing, often times with tears in their eyes expressing how my message of joy has given them hope.

How would you describe your brand? My brand is simply to help people find joy. Psalm 16:11 is the scripture I sign my books with and quote all the time during my presentations: "You will show me the path of life; in your presence is the fullness of joy; at your right hand there are pleasures forevermore."

What is your vision for your business? As a dyed-in-the-wool optimist, I'm always looking for ways to expand my joy brand. In the months and years to come, my business plan includes another book, conferences for women and fabulous destination retreats, all centered around the theme of joy. And some day, maybe not too far off in the distant future, I hope to open a Pockets of Joy boutique.

What would you tell your younger self about entrepreneurship? Fear of the unknown is no reason not to try, but rather exactly why you must go forward, if for no other reason than to conquer fear and WIN!

What would you say is your greatest professional accomplishment to date? My greatest personal accomplishment is raising my son, which is also my greatest joy.

I believe my greatest professional achievement was having the courage to turn an idea into reality, and despite the arduous anxiety-filled process of stepping out on my own, I am proud I answered the call. I am truly humbled and above all grateful to see the positive life-changing impact sharing the concept of joy can have on so many.

Robyne Robinson

fivexfive art consultants
www.fivexfiveart.com

Please describe your business: fivexfive art consultants is an aeronautic term meaning "seeing clearly". Our consulting firm works closely with companies, organizations and artists to build brand identity through public art.

What led your decision to start your business? I began to see how exciting large-scale public art projects were while working as the Art Director at MSP Airport. The idea of collaborating with artists, architects and contractors to create a 21st century airport is astounding.

It is also a big responsibility to help a company brand its identity with the community as a partner. Public art is a shared idea between an organization and the community of who we perceive ourselves to be. fivexfive is adapt at clearly seeing that possibility through to reality..

What keeps you going? What drives you? I'm motivated by the challenge, a passion for what I do, and a fear of failure. I was raised on the belief there's no such thing as failure, but I don't want to find out if there is.

How would you describe your brand? My brand is art networking.

What is your vision for your business? My vision is to be a leader in creating future airports and businesses now.

What would you tell your younger self about entrepreneurship? I'd tell myself, yes getting a paycheck every two weeks is easy. And it's lazy. It means taking someone's BS because they hand you their money. Being your own boss means you can walk away from anything that doesn't respect you, your community or your contributions. When you work hard as an entrepreneur, you savor the success even more.

What would you say is your greatest professional accomplishment to date? My greatest professional accomplishment (after being accepted into the Minnesota Broadcasters' Hall of Fame) has been creating an award-winning arts program at MSP Airport in five years. It has been recognized by Public Art Review, The New York Times, CNBC, Fox News Latino, and my favorite as "One of the 12 Most Beautiful Terminals in the World" by national blog writer The Points Guy (https://thepointsguy.com/2017/08/beautiful-airport-terminals).

"Being your own boss means you can walk away from anything that doesn't respect you, your community or your contributions. When you work hard as an entrepreneur, you savor the success even more."

Sabrina Jones

S & J Creations LLC., DBA Body Love Products
www.bodyloveproducts.com

Please describe your business: S & J Creations LLC., DBA Body Love Products specializes in Shea Butter aromatherapy bath and body products and personal gifts. We offer upscale yet affordable skin care and aromatherapy products to the style conscious consumer focused on health and well-being. Body Love Products mission is to renew and rejuvenate your mind, body and spirt with our natural and handmade products of body butters, scrubs, oils, roller balls and inhalers. Our ultimate endeavor is to provide alternative options in bringing the ultimate Spa experience home.

What led your decision to start your business? As a sufferer of sensitive skin and eczema since I was eight and with more than 3 million US cases per year (source: Mayo Clinic), I knew others could benefit from a quality, affordable product that provides relief from inflammation, irritation, and swelling. I researched Shea Butter, a fat extracted from the nut of the African Shea tree and discovered so many medicinal uses and healing components of vitamins A, E, and F. A focus on health and wellness centered, Shea Butter and aromatherapy, brought Body Love Products to reality in 2015.

What keeps you going? What drives you? Two gems: First, my customers. Customer feedback on how my products helped them and their need for more let's me know, I'm making a difference. Second, my children. As a a wife and mother, my focus is to leave a legacy for my sons by providing a blueprint for them to add their mark. I'm driven by my passion, faith and the love and support of my husband and children to succeed. I'm driven to be fierce, and to slay in this industry while leaving a mark of love and compassion.

How would you describe your brand? Body Love Products makes high quality skin care products accessible and affordable for the stylish conscious consumer focused on loving themselves while resolving issues around stress that can lead to dry skin and other health ailments. Body Love Products reminds us to invest in self-care to be renewed, relaxed and rejuvenated. Hence our slogan, "Hello Beautiful! #Loveyourself!"

What is your vision for your business? In 4th Quarter 2018, we will be Women's Business Enterprise and Women-Owned Small Business Federal Contracting Program certified. This will lead to continued growth and access to diverse suppliers to promote our brand. Whether you are at the local barber shop or hair salon, or major retail store, Body Love Products will be accessible. We believe in philanthropy, educating, and supporting the community. We will continue partnerships that promote awareness on mental and physical health initiatives. A strong mind, body, and partnership, will create healthier & stronger communities.

What would you tell your younger self about entrepreneurship? "You don't make progress by standing on the sidelines, whimpering and complaining. You make progress by implementing ideas" – Shirley Chisholm. Do something that makes you happy. Surround yourself with jewels of mentors, prayer warriors, subject matter experts, optimist's and those that will tell you the truth; with empathy and love. Entrepreneurship will be the biggest adventure to bringing your creative ideas to life. No matter the No's you hear, remember, it takes that one "Yes".

What would you say is your greatest professional accomplishment to date? When we launched our first endeavor was to participate in a Holiday Boutique featuring various vendors located in an upscale Minneapolis shopping mall. The access to that community of clients provided heightened exposure, making us the top-selling vendor. We were very thankful to repeat our success in 2016. The opportunities proved we had a place and most importantly a demand.

49

Shakeeta Sturden

Catwalkfierce Makeup Artistry
facebook.com/catwalkfierce

Please describe your business: I offer makeup services to a wide array of clientele on a freelance basis. My range of services includes: videography, photography bridal, beauty, and editorial. I also travel to clients and provide on location services as requested.

What led your decision to start your business? I became very impatient with the lack of creativity in the corporate sector. It was literally draining me to be in the office every day. I knew I needed to be doing something that provided an outlet for my creativity and could also provide me an income. The journey that followed led me to makeup artistry and my business growing year after year.

What keeps you going? What drives you? My passion for freedom is what keeps me going. Being self-sufficient and in control of how much I make and when I make it is imperative for cooperative economics. I think entrepreneurship is not utilized as much as it could be in the Black community and I want to be an example today and for future generations that your life/career can literally be whatever you make it. If you can see it in your mind, you can achieve it. PERIOD.

How would you describe your brand? My brand is forward, bold, and trendy. I am an equal opportunity brand. Everyone is welcomed here. We believe in social justice and equity in access. We actively fight causes that we believe in and contribute to our community in positive ways that enhance our experience as a community.

What is your vision for your business? My vision is to be the leading makeup/skincare professional in the region. Offering advanced skin services and techniques that accommodate people of color as well as products that combat issues that we experience in general as a result of having a higher melanin content. Eventually I would like to become an ed-ucator in a vocational or technical capacity to underserved youth in urban areas. This will continue the legacy.

What would you tell your younger self about entrepreneurship? It's hard. It's worth it. Don't let anyone else's opinion stop you from pursuing your dreams. As a matter of fact, don't even ask anyone's opinions. It's just noise. Be confident, get skilled at whatever it is and be the best at it. You are your only competition and there is enough wealth for everyone.

What would you say is your greatest professional accomplishment to date? My greatest professional accomplishment to date would be maintaining professional relationships and getting to work with some of the same people and businesses on a consistent basis. I enjoy what I do and I love when I have executed a project and demonstrated my skill so well that people want to work with me again. Other than imitation, retention is the highest compliment.

"Being self-sufficient and in control of how much I make and when I make it is imperative for cooperative economics."

Taneika Williams

NeikasBeauty
www.neikasbeauty.com

Please describe your business: NeikasBeauty is a professional freelance luxury makeup service specializing in bridal, fashion and events.

What led your decision to start your business? Would you believe it if I told you I was a tom boy growing up? It wasn't until 9th grade that I began to take an interest in beauty. During my high school years, I was all about hair. In 2008 I started to get into makeup. This started as just a hobby watching YouTube videos for hours at a time. One day I thought it would be fun to try it. So, I went out and bought some makeup and attempted to recreate what I've watched numerous of times. I loved how makeup made me feel. It was therapeutic.

I love art and makeup is a form of art. After helping some of my first clients I knew it was something I wanted to further. The more I picked up makeup brushes and products, the more I fell in love with it. Seeing my clients walk away with smiles on their faces, with that extra boost of confidence shining through, makes me happy. I decided to start Neikas-Beauty- beauty that comes in all colors by enhancing natural beauty one face at a time!

What keeps you going? What drives you? My daughter and my clients keep me going. Being able to show my daughter that no matter where you start you can reach that goal you set. I am motivated by my clients excitement after being in my chair. Their words of encouragement and prayers definitely make it possible for me to propel forward. Being able to be creative and learn new things drives me.

How would you describe your brand? I would describe my brand as a professional luxury service. When you book with me It's more than a makeup appointment, but a meaningful experience!

What is your vision for your business? My vision for my business is to have a one stop shop lounge for all your beauty needs.

What would you tell your younger self about entrepreneurship? I would tell my younger self to go after what I wanted earlier rather than later. Chase your dream and don't allow anything to stand in your way. Not a job, friends nor family. Trust your gut feeling, it's often right. Lastly Invest in yourself!

What would you say is your greatest professional accomplishment to date? I would say my greatest professional accomplishment would be maintaining a professional brand for myself and also continuing to take the necessary trainings/courses to help with my brand.

"Seeing my clients walk away with smiles on their faces, with that extra boost of confidence shining through, makes me happy."

Desireé L. Wells

DASH Collective
www.dash-collective.com

Please describe your business: The DASH Collective is dedicated to creating purposeful, unique designs and projects that esteems the genuine heart behind my business. The tools to accomplish this have evolved over the years, but my enduring passion to inspire and bridge through creativity remains unchanged. As a creative boutique, the DASH Collective specializes in translating what's in your mind and heart into an authentic visual story, while connecting to your dream client and taking your business to the next level. This is mastered through innovative design services including photography, branding, graphic and website design.

What led your decision to start your business? I founded the DASH Collective while working full-time as a corporate creative and marketing director. Upon hearing numerous of stories from passionate business owners and entrepreneurs who were relentless in their endeavors but were unsuccessful conveying their passions and ideas to the world. I became convicted and knew that my purpose was to extend my artistic ingenuity to others outside of the traditional corporate world. This is accomplished through the inspiring designs I create to tell their brand's true story.

What keeps you going? What drives you? Some people are fueled by coffee; I am powered by my talents and heart's desire to create! Branding can mean a lot of different things. As for me, it is the foundation of your business. It is how you blend who you are with the work that you do. I love to help business owners build powerful visuals that not only reflect who they are, but also connects to their dream clients and elevates their business.

How would you describe your brand? My brand is me; - Authentic. Creative. Happy. Thoughtful. Inspired. The DASH Collective is the perfect blend of my unique set of gifts, my personality, my sense of humor, my beliefs, and most importantly, my heart. Everything I do is infused with a passion for design. With a heart that's driven to create, genuinely connect and help inspiring individuals and businesses, I count myself very blessed to be doing what I love.

What is your vision for your business? To change and empower the community using the power of design. As a "creativepreneur" (creative + entrepreneur) collaborating with inspiring people, crafting meaningful designs and cultivating creativity truly is my passion. The DASH Collective is on a mission to help businesses make an impact by equipping them with purpose-driven designs. Every business deserves powerful and authentic design, that includes start-up entrepreneurs, long-time industry leaders, independent artisans, purpose-driven organizations or mom-and-pop shops. Every visual aspect and message shared should tell the story of the passion and person(s) behind the brand and the soul of the business, boldly and honestly.

What would you tell your younger self about entrepreneurship? The Most High has a specific calling on your life. It may not be the same as those around you. You will never walk into what He has for you chasing another person's purpose. Be you. Be obedient to what He has commanded of you. God equates obedience with success.

What would you say is your greatest professional accomplishment to date? The ability to help people envision their dreams for their business and bring them to reality has been my greatest professional accomplishment. Each day may be different and present challenges, but the reward is far greater as I get to build people up through the power of creative, design innovation.

Tashonda Brown

Tashonda S. Brown
www.tashondasbrown.com

Please describe your business: My business is focused on the enhancing women's beauty in every area of life. Mind, body and soul. Connecting and identifying with who you are and what makes you uniquely you using my gifts and talents of hair and makeup.

What led your decision to start your business? I believe that the vision and the gifts provided to me has pushed me into this industry. I never seen myself as a hairstylist or a makeup artist growing up. But I always enjoyed doing it. My grandmother saw the gift in me and told me to pursue it.

What keeps you going? What drives you? The things that keep me going are meeting and connecting with new women. Hearing their stories and having the ability to compliment their lives with enhancing their beauty. My children and my family drive me to reach higher heights and deeper depths to accomplish and acquire more goals. Also, given the opportunity to be the ultimate example of a woman to my daughters and my son.

How would you describe your brand? I would describe my brand as chic, modern and matchless. I believe my talent is unique and can't be compared to anyone else but me!

What is your vision for your business? I see my business expanding in the future into a brick and mortar. Providing exclusive makeup classes and courses online and in person. Teaching women the beauty they have within themselves. Wakening their confidence and self-esteem not only with using temporary enhancements like hair and makeup but impacting the many lives I connect with.

What would you tell your younger self about entrepreneurship? Believe in you! Everything you have is within you! Don't look to the right or to the left but your help comes from above! Fear is only a dream killer and a time consumer!

What would you say is your greatest professional accomplishment to date? I would say my greatest professional accomplishment to date is having my work being featured in national magazines, commercials and movies. I don't take any opportunity or any encounter that I have lightly. Every person I have met on my journey has imparted a greater confidence and awareness in me which keeps me going! And to let me know I am on the right path!

"I believe that the vision and the gifts provided to me has pushed me into this industry. I believe my talent is unique and can't be compared to anyone else but me!"

Thank You

The work of Fearless Commerce has continued because of great partners and investors. We thank each of you for your faith and support!

Investors:

Platinum

 Knight Foundation

Gold

TCIA   The Twin Cities Innovation Alliance

4RM+ULA   4RM+ULA Architects

Silver

GRAY PLANT MOOTY   Gray, Plant & Mooty

5QIS   5QIS, LLC

Photo Shoot Venue:
Stacy Anderstrom, CREED Interactive
www.creedinteractive.com

Photographers:
Andrea Allen Reed, www.andreaellenreed.com
Desiree Benton Wells, www.dash-collective.com

Stylists:
Char Dobbs, www.charstyleandimage.com
Morgan A. Wider, www.widerstyle.com

Make-up Artists:
Tanieka Williams, www.neikasbeauty.com
Shakeeta Sturden, facebook/catwalkfierce
Tashonda S. Brown, www.tashondasbrown.com

CPSIA information can be obtained
at www.ICGtesting.com
Printed in the USA
LVHW071814131218
600348LV00005B/75/P